THE
TREE
THAT'S MEANT TO BE

Dedicated to
the forest

All rights reserved. Published in the United States by Doubleday, an imprint of
Random House Children's Books, a division of Penguin Random House LLC, New York.
Published simultaneously in the United Kingdom by
Oxford University Press, Oxford, in 2019.

Doubleday and the colophon are registered trademarks of
Penguin Random House LLC.

Visit us on the Web! rhcbooks.com

Educators and librarians, for a variety of teaching tools,
visit us at RHTeachersLibrarians.com

Library of Congress Cataloging-in-Publication Data is available upon request.
ISBN 978-0-593-11967-9 (trade)

MANUFACTURED IN CHINA
10 9 8 7 6 5 4 3 2 1
First American Edition

THE TREE
THAT'S MEANT TO BE

YUVAL ZOMMER

Doubleday Books for Young Readers

I
am
the tree
that's meant to be.

I started life as a tiny seed,
but soon enough
it was plain to see
that I was never, ever going to be
a perfect, grown-up tree!

I branched a bit to the left,
too much to the right,
and didn't really focus on my height.

While other trees
grew poised and tall,
I lagged behind.

Looking different.
Feeling small.

Spring,

summer,

autumn.

Seasons came, stayed, and went.

Then one harsh, cold winter night,
the forest turned . . .

. . . snowy white.

The people came with
measuring tapes and saws,

searching for a flawless tree.
A Christmas tree to cut and take indoors.

Soon, one by one,
the other trees were gone.
It was just me now.

Alone.

I shivered, I shuddered.

"I–i–i–is anyone there?"
I stuttered into the night.

But who would hear my cry?
Who could speak the language of tree?
And *understand* me?

And then, at dawn,
foxes,
deer,
and birds.
They had heard!

Everyone brought
berries, feathers,
nuts, and flowers.

They dressed me for hours and hours
until I was a jolly, festive tree.

"Hello! Hello!"
"Welcome, squirrel.
Greetings, bear!"
Laughter filled the air.

My clearing rang with
Christmas cheer.

As darkness fell, a shooting star dropped down.

It sank into my branches and shone so pure,
so bright, that I became a **tree of light.**

Among the creatures great and small,
I felt loved.
I felt tall!

Seasons came, stayed, and went.
I am no longer alone.
This is my forest home.

Through wind and rain,
sun and snow, I grow.

Always here, ever green.

I
am
the tree
that's meant to be.